Sarah Bee works as an author, journalist, and editor in London.
The Yes is her debut picture book.

Satoshi Kitamura has illustrated over sixty children's books. One
of his recent titles, *Millie's Marvellous Hat* (Andersen Press USA), was a
2010 Kate Greenaway Medal shortlist book. He currently lives in Japan.

For M&J,

because yes.

S.B.

Text © 2014 Sarah Bee
Illustrations © 2014 Satoshi Kitamura
All rights reserved

First published in Great Britain in 2014 by Andersen Press Ltd., 20 Vauxhall Bridge Road, London SW1V 2SA
This edition published in 2015 by Eerdmans Books for Young Readers, an imprint of Wm. B. Eerdmans Publishing Co.

William B. Eerdmans Publishing Co.
2140 Oak Industrial Dr. NE, Grand Rapids, Michigan 49505
P.O. Box 163, Cambridge CB3 9PU U.K.
www.eerdmans.com/youngreaders
ISBN 978-0-8028-5449-0

Color separated in Switzerland by Photolitho AG, Zürich
Printed and bound in Malaysia by Tien Wah Press in September 2014, first printing
21 20 19 18 17 16 15   9 8 7 6 5 4 3 2 1
A catalog listing for this book is available from the Library of Congress.

Sarah Bee   Satoshi Kitamura

the Yes

EERDMANS BOOKS FOR YOUNG READERS

GRAND RAPIDS, MICHIGAN • CAMBRIDGE, U.K.

In a soft comfy nest in a safe warm place there snoozed a great big orange thing called the Yes. He was snug, but the Yes had a Where to go to.

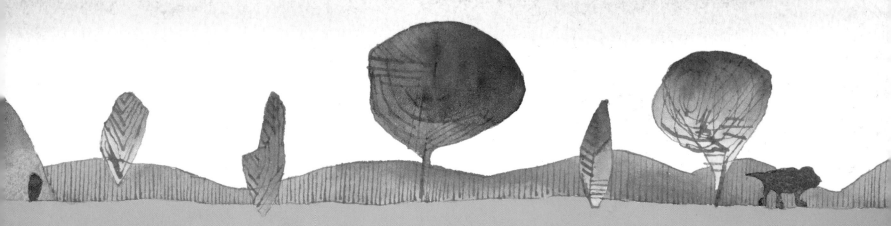

So he left his nest and went trundling out to see.

The Where was an endless place of Nos. The Nos were everywhere and everywhat in swarms and flocks and packs. They teemed and seethed. They picked and nipped and snipped and snicked.

They were so many and so very that you could see nothing but Nos. They made all the Here and all the Else a no-ness and a not-ness.

The Yes came to a tree. The tree was tall. It had fruit.
The Yes was hungry.

Yes?

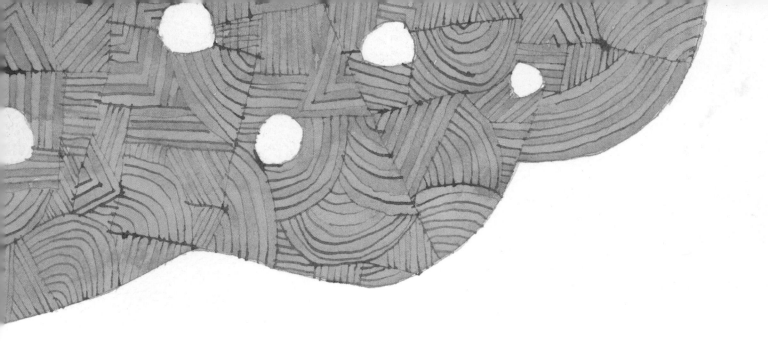

Was the tree too tall to climb?
The Yes was big and lumpen.

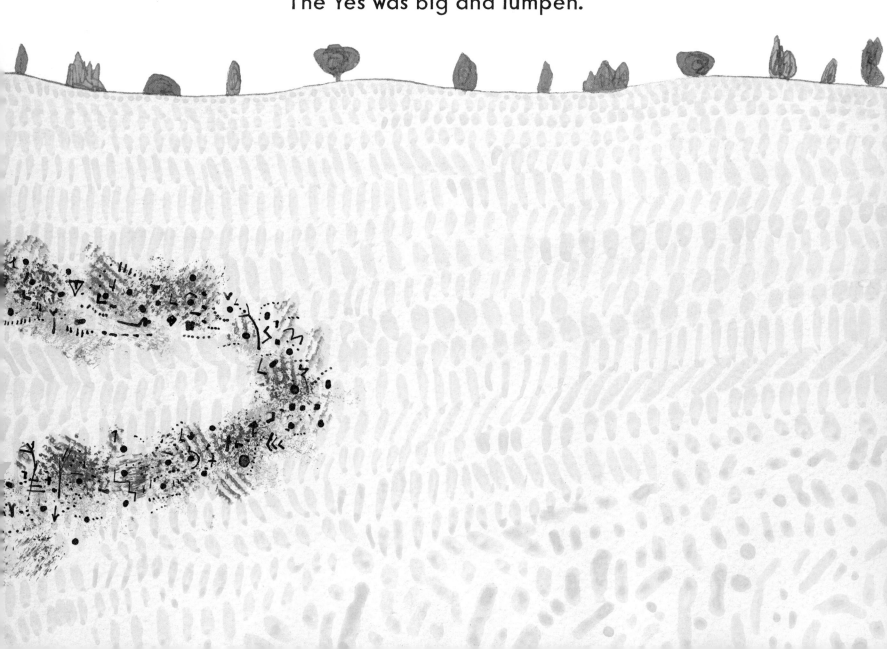

The Nos swarmed around the Yes in a thick cloud of
no and said all the nos there ever were.

"No, too big."

"No, too tall."

"No, too silly."

"No, you'll fall."

NO!

The Nos sat on the Yes and stood on his head and pulled
his ears and tugged his tail. They made such a huge no that
you could hear it from the sky and feel it in the ground.

But the Nos were small and the Yes was large. The Nos were flimsy and the Yes was bulky. The Nos were not a thing, and the Yes was a great big thing.

The Yes looked . . .
and climbed the tree.

Yes!

Yes?

The Yes lumbered on.

In a thereish part of the great big Where,
he came to a valley. It had a bridge.
A little flimsy bridge.
The Yes was big and hefty.

Yes?

The Nos came and rained down no all over.

There were Nos in the air, Nos by his feet, Nos in his fur, Nos up his nose.

"NO!" said the Nos.

It is what Nos do and what they are.

"No, you couldn't.

It's too rickety."

"No, you shouldn't.
It's too trickety."

"You will break it.

You won't make it."

NO!

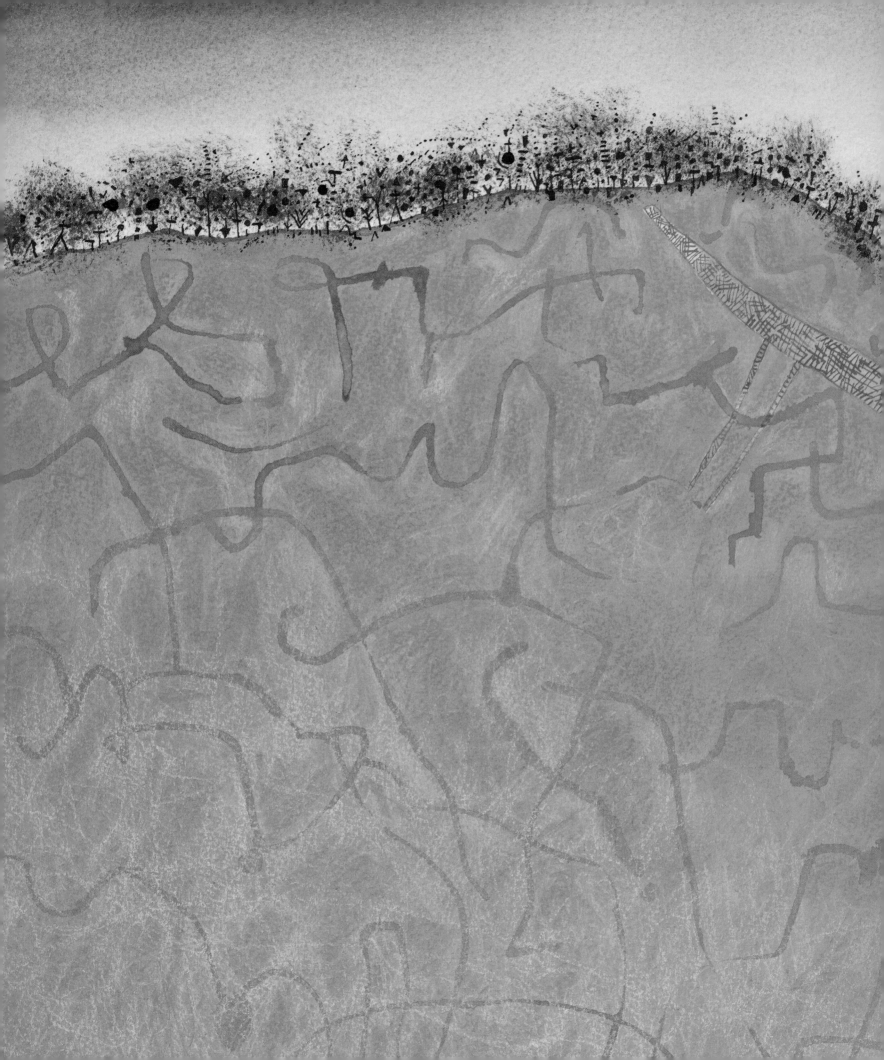

The song of the Nos was loud and long and so full of
no that there was nothing else to hear.

The Yes looked . . .

Yes!

The Yes bumbled on.

In a further part of the big wide Where, he came to a river.

Yes?

"No, no, no, it's much too deep!"

"No, no, no, it's far too steep!"

"No, beware!"

"No, don't dare!"

NO!

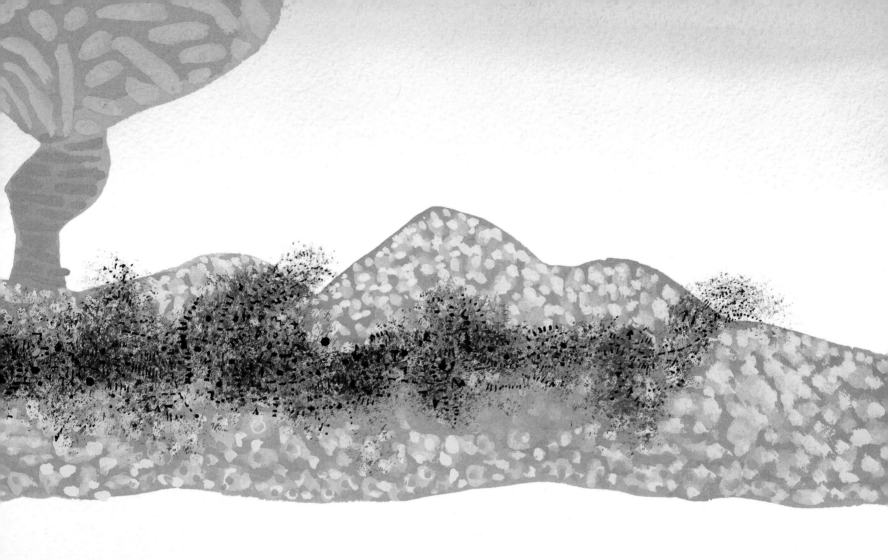

The Nos put up a wall of no that went all
around the Where and into all the This
until everything was full of no.

The Yes looked . . .

The Yes gumbled on, and after a When he came to a scary dark wood in the Where.

"No no no no no no no NO NO NO!"

The Yes rumbled on and on.
He went scrumbling by the marshes and flundering through the fields.

He went over the rocks and bumps and dips, into and out of the wide empty spaces, over and under the bad barren places.

The Nos noed and noed and noed in numbers no one could count.
The Yes only yessed in all his goodness and **bigness** and **yesness.**

And then the Yes came to a big rolling hill. The Nos did the loudest and no-ing-est no they could do. But all the Nos in all the Where all put together were only a no in the end. A no made of dust and nothing that wasn't ever really there at all.

The Yes went **up,** and **up,**

until the noise of the Nos in their no-ness and not-ness grew
smaller
and smaller,
and fainter
and fainter,

until there was no more no and never had been.

There was only **the Yes.**

Yes!

Wisdom Tales in an imprint of World Wisdom, Inc.

For Jonathan, who knows the spirit of the cheetah.—KLW
In memory of my brother Roblay Khadar and to my beloved homeland, Somalia.—KM
For Anne Bosley, the very best of friends.—JC

Library of Congress Cataloging-in-Publication

Names: Williams, Karen Lynn, author. | Mohammed, Khadra, author. | Cairns, Julia, illustrator.
Title: Spirit of the cheetah : a Somali tale / by Karen Lynn Williams & Khadra Mohammed ;
illustrated by Julia Cairns.
Description: Bloomington, Indiana : Wisdom Tales, [2021] | Audience: Ages 4-8 | Audience: Grades 2-3 |
Summary: To win the race that will prove he is a man, young Roblay runs constantly through his Somali
village, until his grandfather advises him to capture the spirit of the mighty Shabelle River.
Includes facts about cheetahs.
Identifiers: LCCN 2020027466 (print) | LCCN 2020027467 (ebook) | ISBN
9781937786854 (hardcover) | ISBN 9781937786861 (epub)
Subjects: CYAC: Running--Fiction. | Coming of age--Fiction. | Shebeli River
(Ethiopia and Somalia)--Fiction. | Cheetah--Fiction. | Somalia--Fiction.
Classification: LCC PZ7.W66655 Spi 2021 (print) | LCC PZ7.W66655 (ebook) |
DDC 813.5--dc23
LC record available at https://lccn.loc.gov/2020027466
LC ebook record available at https://lccn.loc.gov/2020027467

Printed in China on acid-free paper.

For information address Wisdom Tales,
P.O. Box 2682, Bloomington, Indiana, 47402-2682
www.wisdomtalespress.com

Spirit of the Cheetah

A Somali Tale

By Karen Lynn Williams
& Khadra Mohammed

Illustrated by Julia Cairns

✦Wisdom Tales✦

Author Notes

In the Somali language the word *shabelle* is used interchangeably for leopard and cheetah. But it is the cheetah for which the Shabelle River is named. The cheetah is distinguishable from the leopard by the teardrop markings around its eyes, and by its sleek build it is the fastest land animal in the world. The Shabelle River also runs with great speed and force. At one time Somalia was known for the large number of cheetahs that roamed the countryside. Today the cheetah is considered an endangered species across Africa. Vulnerable to loss of habitat, war, famine, and poaching for sale as pets and for their skins, this magnificent animal is at risk of becoming extinct worldwide.

—*Karen Lynn Williams*

My family was forced to leave Somalia when Siad Barre came to power in 1969, the year I was born. As a result I was born in exile. It was a difficult choice my parents made, to leave and never be able to return to our homeland. I have traveled to many countries around the world growing up, but I am forbidden to even visit Somalia. As a child I longed for my native home and a place to belong. I spent endless days listening to my father as he told tales about the beautiful land and the people who lived peacefully with the animals, drawing much wisdom from them. These stories gave me a great pride and comfort. Thousands of Somalis have left their country, now torn apart and barren as the result of civil war and famine. I hope one day to be able to journey back to the one place I think of as home, a land of pride and story, the land of the Shabelle River where the cheetah once roamed in plenty.

—*Khadra Mohammed*

R oblay ran to the market to buy mangoes. Willy-
nilly, he knocked over a stack of firewood.
"Why must you run?" the angry wood seller yelled.

"I am practicing for the big race."
Roblay ran to the well to fetch water. Bumpety-bumpety
the water sloshed out of his bucket.
"Why must you always run?" Mother yelled.
"I will run the big race and prove I am a man."

Each day Roblay ran and ran. He ran right through the seven rocks game his friends played.

"Why must you always run?" they called after him.

"Only the fastest three in the big race will be declared men. I will be one of them."

Dawn of the big race came. An endless line of boys stood at the starting line. Roblay was among them. The wise one lowered his arm, the signal to begin.

Roblay ran faster than he had ever run before. He ran as fast as a camel. But he was not one of the first three to finish the race. He walked home slowly with Awoowo, his grandfather.

"I have run my best," he said. "How will I ever be among the first three?"

"Get some rest," Awoowo answered. "Come tonight and I will tell you."

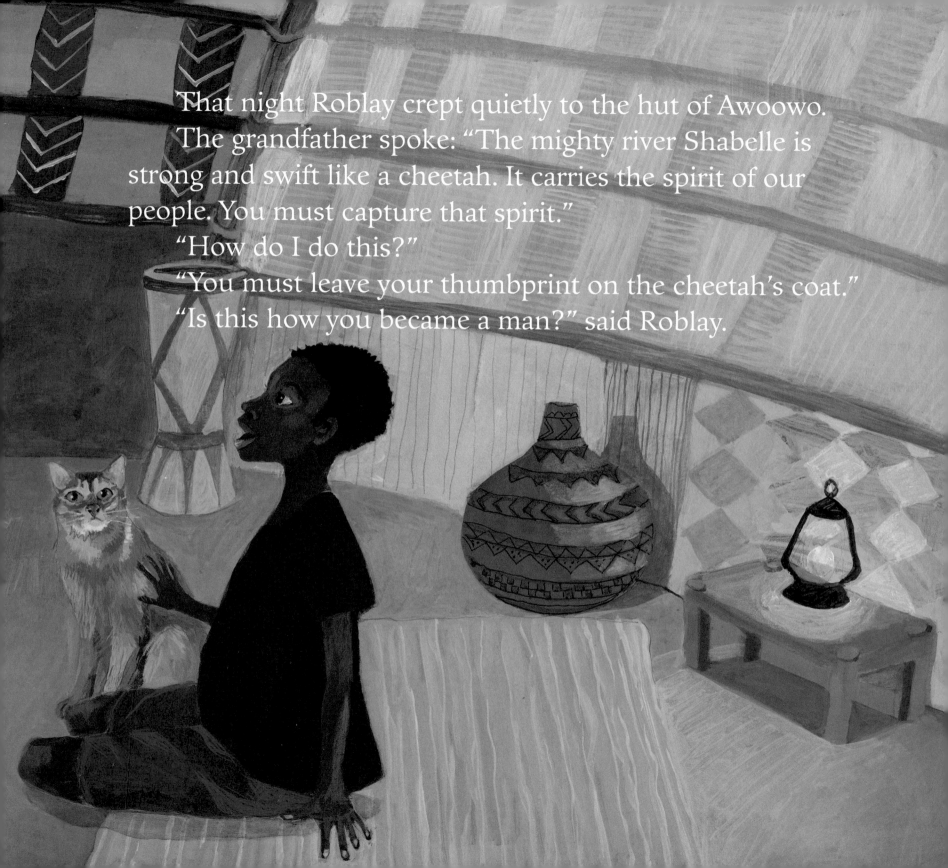

That night Roblay crept quietly to the hut of Awoowo.

The grandfather spoke: "The mighty river Shabelle is strong and swift like a cheetah. It carries the spirit of our people. You must capture that spirit."

"How do I do this?"

"You must leave your thumbprint on the cheetah's coat."

"Is this how you became a man?" said Roblay.

Awoowo nodded. "Long ago the earth was green with plentiful rain. There was no hunger, no war. Many cheetahs, swiftest of all animals, roamed our land.

"Our people named the mighty river Shabelle after the cheetah. His power unites our clans and carries the thumb-prints of all those who have proven themselves as men."

Roblay spent days searching for even one cheetah in the hot dry lands along the Shabelle River.

Finally he spotted a mother and her cubs across the powerful river. The cubs tumbled over each other in play. Their coats were yellow, without spots.

Roblay went back to Awoowo. "Does it matter if the cheetah I mark with my thumb is a cub?" Awoowo laughed so hard he nearly fell backwards.

"Are you to remain a cub?" he asked.

Roblay returned to the Shabelle River and watched. He waited for the cheetah to move, sleek and strong.

With the waiting, Roblay grew patient.

He studied the movements of the cheetah and so he learned to move with grace.

Roblay ran alongside the cheetah, always keeping the mighty river between them and so he too grew to be swift.

Like the cheetah's padded paws his bare, calloused feet
hardly touched the ground. His muscles grew sleek.

But the year until the next race was nearly over and Roblay still had not left his thumbprint on the cheetah's coat. "I have failed," he thought.

Early on the morning of the big race, Roblay went one more time to the great Shabelle. He watched as the cheetah waited and then as she ran with power and the swiftness of flight and overcame her prey. She had given all her strength to that one short race and lay down to rest.

And so Roblay dove into the great river and swam steadily across the current. The cheetah stood up and watched.

Roblay reached the bank of the river and climbed out. His heart beat with fear. The cheetah's heart pounded with equal speed. Slowly Roblay raised his hand, shiny with the water of the great river.

He searched for a place on the cheetah's coat and pressed his thumb against the sleek fur along with the thumbprints of all those who had become men before him.

The animal rose and sniffed Roblay. They held each other's eyes and then slowly Roblay walked backwards to the great river.

He swam across to his village and he drank from a calabash, the camel milk his mother had prepared. He walked straight and tall to the starting place.

Spectators came from every
village in the region. With them stood
Awoowo, his eyes fixed on Roblay as the cheetah
had fixed her eyes on him. The wise one gave the signal.
    Roblay began to run and with each step he remembered
the beauty and grace of the cheetah. He felt the strength of
the great river, Shabelle. With patience he kept a steady pace.

The sun rose high above the land and just before the
crest of the final hill, Roblay called on the spirit of Shabelle.
His bare feet flew above the ground.

In the final charge to the finish he was weightless. And when the race was over, there he was in third place among the winners!

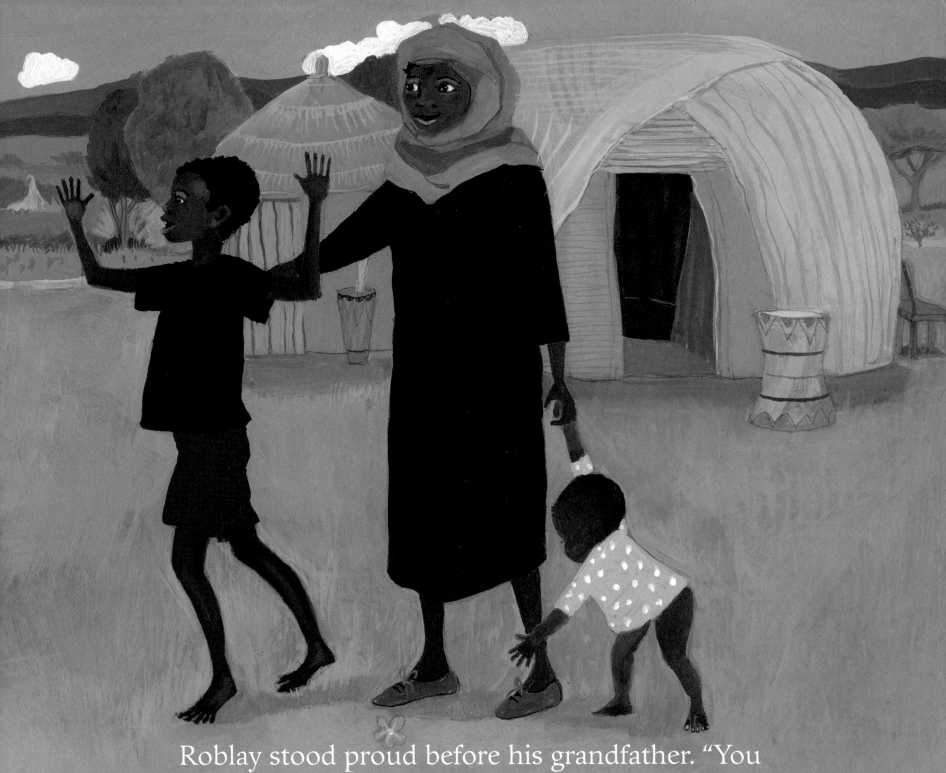

Roblay stood proud before his grandfather. "You became a man even before the race began," Awoowo said.

Notes on the Cheetah

✯ The English word *cheetah* is derived from the Sanskrit *citra*, meaning "adorned or painted," referring to the distinctive black spots on the cheetah's yellow coat.

✯ The cheetah, whose scientific name is *Acinonyx jubatus*, is a large cat of the subfamily *Felinae*, which occurs today in North, Southern, and East Africa, and also in parts of Iran.

✯ Historically the cheetah ranged throughout Africa and across vast stretches of Asia, from the Arabian Peninsula in the west to the Indian subcontinent in the east.

✯ In ancient Egypt the cheetah was revered as a symbol of royalty in the form of the cat goddess Mafdet, whose name means "swift runner."

✯ The cheetah has lived in association with humans since at least 3000 BCE, when the Sumerians depicted a leashed cheetah on an official seal.

✯ The cheetah is the fastest land animal on earth, capable of reaching speeds of up to 75 miles (120 kilometers) per hour. It can go from 0-60 miles (0-95 kilometers) an hour in just three seconds.

✮ The cheetah is perfectly adapted for running at high speeds: its legs are proportionally longer than other big cats; it has an elongated spine that increases stride length; it has unretractable claws and special paw pads for extra traction; and it has a long tail for balance and rapid direction change.

✮ Unlike other big cats, the cheetah is a daytime hunter, relying on its exceptional speed, keen eyesight, and camouflaged spotted coat for success.

✮ Cheetah cubs often play with other cubs by tapping their back legs when running and tripping them over, a skill that they later use when hunting prey.

✮ The global cheetah population living in the wild today is estimated at around 7,000, sharply down from approximately 100,000 in the year 1900.

✮ The main reasons for the decline in the cheetah population are: habitat encroachment, poaching, illegal pet trade, vehicle collision, and conflict with humans, especially over livestock.

✮ The cheetah is currently red-listed as "vulnerable" by the International Union for Conservation of Nature (IUCN), meaning that it is at high risk of endangerment in the wild.